James G. Burnett

Love and Laughter

Being a legacy of rhyme

James G. Burnett

Love and Laughter
Being a legacy of rhyme

ISBN/EAN: 9783337266738

Printed in Europe, USA, Canada, Australia, Japan

Cover: Foto ©Andreas Hilbeck / pixelio.de

More available books at **www.hansebooks.com**

James G. Burnett.

Love and Laughter

Being A Legacy
of Rhyme

BY

James G. Burnett

––––––

PUBLISHED IN NEW YORK & LONDON
BY G. P. PUTNAM'S SONS
1895

The Knickerbocker Press, New Rochelle, N. Y.

PREFACE AND SKETCH OF THE AUTHOR.

In other years, long passed away, it was my privilege to number among my friends that winning gentleman and versatile and accomplished actor, Mr. James G. Burnett, whom persons familiar with theatrical history will remember as an excellent representative of humorous old men and of eccentric characters in general. He died in 1870, leaving a widow and two sons, the eldest of whom was the author of the verses which have been collected into this volume. I have been asked to write an introductory word, indicative that this is a memorial book, and expressive of the motive that has prompted its publication.

There is but little to be said. It is the old story, of a life of rich promise, blighted almost at its beginning ; of buoyant and radiant youth, suddenly summoned from the threshold of achievement and enjoyment ; of mental power, moral worth, hope, ambition, and happiness darkened, defeated, and extinguished by early death. The annals of literature abound with records of this sad order : the libraries are almost as thickly strewn with relics of youthful talent prematurely destroyed as the beaches are with shells and pebbles when the receding tides have left them bare. To youthful eyes such anomalies of experience seem altogether disastrous, deplorable, and without compensation ; but those observers for whom the evening of life is drawing near are able to see widely, and, if not to understand, at least to feel, that in the mysterious ordainment and conduct of human destiny there is a larger kindness and wisdom than that of man. The only possible comment is the comparatively trite one, that there must be a wider scene than this world, wherein the hopes inspired and the purposes fore-shadowed here are answered and fulfilled. The author of this book was more brilliant and auspicious than anything that he has written ; he died before his mind had in all respects matured, and before his distinctive literary work had been completely begun ; and this selection from his fugitive writings is published by the mother who dearly loved him,—and whom he dearly loved and deeply honored,—to commemorate her singer, and to ask for him the place that he coveted among the kindly, sportive writers of his native land.

The life of this young author was as placid as his equable character, and it was uneventful. He was born in New York, August 5, 1868, and he died at San Antonio, Texas, in the twenty-sixth year of his age, April 20, 1894, and was buried at Greenwood. At seventeen he entered the National University Law School, at Washington, from which institution, in 1887, he was graduated with honors ; and subsequently, after a period of study and preparation, in the law-office of a New York attorney, he formed a partnership with Mr. Henry C. Bryan, his classmate and friend, and formally devoted himself to the practice of that profession. He was successful as a lawyer, almost from the earliest step,—clear in his perceptions, logical in his reasoning, expeditious, direct, impressive, and sincere,—but he soon wore out his strength, in the labor that he loved, and he then was obliged to travel, in the quest of health. From an early age he evinced the impulse to write, and, although he did not follow the literary art as a serious vocation, he was passionately fond of it, and, under more favorable circumstances he might have given himself wholly to its service. As things were, he had made a different choice, and if he wrote at all he wrote casually, according to his fitful moods and fancies ; but to the last he never quite laid down the pen. The quatrain with which this book closes,—simply expressive of sweet and patient resignation and of the ecstacy of sublime faith,—was composed a few days before he died.

The vein in which he chiefly loved to write was that of humorous playfulness, touched with sentiment,—a vein of which, in English literature, the most brilliant representatives are Thomas Hood and Winthrop Mackworth Praed. His characteristic literary manner was waggish, sprightly, sometimes gently satirical, but mostly home-like and prone to domestic themes. His fancy was moved by the thought of a pretty face, by a sense of the frolicsome propensities and whimsicalities of youth, by innocent feminine absurdities, by the contrast—always striking —between life's realities and youth's romantic illusions, and by natural beauty. He was, in personality, honorable, chivalrous, buoyant, gleeful, affectionate, and gentle ; he lived with simplicity and died with composure ; and this book,—in which every trait is genial and every thought is pure, and of which the style is happy with vivacious feeling and verbal grace,—will commend itself to good hearts, wherever it may come.

WILLIAM WINTER.

FORT HILL, NEW BRIGHTON,
STATEN ISLAND, October 22, 1895.

CONTENTS.

vii

NOTE.

Many of the verses included in this volume have appeared in *The Century, Harper's Magazine, The New England Magazine, The Overland Monthly, The Californian, Life, Puck, Judge, Truth, Vogue, The Club,* and other periodicals. Acknowledgment is hereby made for kind permission to reprint.

,

LOVE AND LAUGHTER.

When most by Reason I am sought,
    With graver themes, ofttimes
My foolish Fancy turns to naught,
    And runs to making rhymes.

LOVE AND LAUGHTER.

THE JESTERS.

TIS strange, and yet in all the tales
   Of love and glory that are told,
Of ancient Kings, and royal courts,
   Or old Crusaders brave and bold,

My fancy does not dwell upon
   The ladies of those olden times,
Nor on the knights who loved them then,
   But on the men who wrote their rhymes :

The motley fool, with nimble wit
   And ever quick and ready tongue ;
On all his quips and jokes and jests,
   And all the merry songs he sung.

And if the Buddhist bards be right,
   And it be true that souls of men
Return from Paradise, to walk,
   In mortal form, this earth again,

I know where those old jesters' souls
　　The most congenial life would find ;
And, as I write, I seem to know
　　A hundred of them in my mind.

In patent leather shoes they walk,
　　Instead of pointed slippers, now ;
And in the place of cap and bells,
　　A modern hat adorns the brow.

A coat of latest cut succeeds
　　The ruffled doublet known of yore,
And long creased trousers take the place
　　Of gayly-colored hose they wore.

But still their hearts are warm and true,
　　As when they played their pranks and capers ;
And some you 'll find upon the stage,
　　And some write rhymes for comic papers.

SIXTEEN.

Lyra, you have all the pleasures
                Youth can hold :
Do not think the Future's treasures
                All are gold.
Many gems we call the rarest
                Are not bright :
Future days that look the fairest
                Lose their light.

Be you very slow in letting
                Girlhood pass.
Age will mourn its quick forgetting
                Youth, alas !
Love can wait another season ;
                Until then,
Think you more of books and reason
                Than of men.

Though your sisters smile, disdaining
                All your grace,
In a while you will be reigning
                In their place.

Men will then be just as witty,
                    Never fear ;
They will find you quite as pretty,
                    And as dear.

To you they will come a-wooing
                    Many times ;
Many others, as I 'm doing,
                    Write you rhymes.
Even now one doth adore you,
                    Do not doubt ;
All the more that they ignore you,
                    As not " out."

And when all your love and duty
                    One shall own,—
All your gentleness and beauty
                    His alone,—
Then you may, perchance, discover,
                    Then may know
That he was your girlhood's lover,
                    Long ago.

ST. VALENTINE'S DAY.

Long I wished a messenger,
    All my thoughts to bear,—
Love I could not speak myself ;
    Words I did not dare,
Till I knelt before the shrine
Of the old St. Valentine.

"Good St. Valentine," I said,
    "I have heard men say
Thou wilt furnish messengers
    Of the heart to-day.
If such power be really thine,
Help me, oh, St. Valentine ! "

Then he promised straight to send
    One both fleet and true,—
Such a one as I would have
    Bear my love to you.
But he failed me.   Yes, in fine,
He was false—St. Valentine.

7

So I come, Love, with the hope
   That I dared not speak :
So I tell you of my love,
   Though the words are weak.
Must I all my hopes resign,
Helped not by St. Valentine?

Though the message comes not in
   Style to suit the day,
Yet the heart is full of love
   That the lips can't say.
Don't refuse it, Sweetheart mine !
Be my own true Valentine !

MAIDENS' LOVE.

As Cupid walked abroad one day
  With merry thoughts beguiled,
He passed a grassy knoll, where lay
  A maid who dreamed and smiled.

And to the maiden straight he cried,
  "Now, by my mother's dove,
Why smilest thou?" The maid replied,
  "I slept, and dreamed of love."

But even as she spoke, the wight
  With laughter drew his dart,
And like a bird it winged its flight
  Straight to the maiden's heart.

"To dream of love you have no need,"
  In triumph Cupid cried;
"Know now the thrill of love indeed,"
  And as he spoke, she sighed.

And from that time down unto this,
  The fact no one denies,—
A maiden's dreams of love are bliss,
  But when she loves she sighs.

MY NEW SWEETHEART.

FAREWELL to all the girls I 've known,
  Whate'er their names or stations ;
To Winter suppers, Summer walks,
  And all the old flirtations.

A new one takes their places now,
  Surpassing all the others ;
And feelings that I had for them
  Were only like a brother's.

She 's all that 's pure, and good, and true,
  And all that 's sweet and winning ;
And with the love I 've found for her
  A new life is beginning.

She is as fair as lilies are,
  Her hand is like a fairy's,
Her touch as light as thistledown,
  Her soul as pure as Mary's.

Her clear blue eyes have never known
  The power that lies within them,
Nor has she ever thought that men
  Might some day die to win them.

No thought of conquest has this maid,
  No fond hearts has she broken,
Nor has she ever said one word
  That she could wish unspoken !

Her name ? Who is she, do you ask ?
  And will I tell you ? Maybe.
Oh, yes ; of course I will. Now laugh—
  She 's just my sister's baby !

LEGAL MEDITATIONS.

WHAT use to me is " Byles on Bills " ?
For " Jarman on the Law of Wills "
    I would n't give a jackstone.
Nor would I give another for
" Juries and Jury Trials," nor
Coke, Bacon, Parsons, Story, or
    Fearne, Chitty, Kent, or Blackstone.

Will Byles help me to pay the bill .
I owe for flowers ? Can *her* will
    Be changed by reading Jarman ?
What 's " Greenleaf's Evidence " to me ?—
Or Littleton ? or Parker ?—he
Is drier than theosophy,—
    Yes, worse than any Brahmin.

And " Kneeland on Attachments," too,
Has nothing in it that will do—
    The title is misleading.
And though through dusty books I read,
Alas, I ne'er can learn to plead
In Cupid's Court, so she will heed,
    From " Stephen's Rules of Pleading."

"Collyer on Partnership" I 've read,
And vainly too ; "Contracts to Wed,"
　　By some one named Fitzsimmon.
Nor does it seem to help me on,
That "Marriage Settlements" I con,
Or Schouler's learned book upon
　　"The Law of Married Women."

There is no statute I can find
Will make a maiden change her mind ;
　　Nor know I where the place is
To find a law to help me win
A suit like mine,—or I 'd begin
To search it out.　It is n't in
　　My set of "Leading Cases."

But—"Baylies on Appeals !"　Ah, there
Is just the answer to my prayer !
　　I know now how to do it.
From her decision—by the Seal
Of all the Courts !—I will appeal ;
And that will make the verdict *nil*
　　Until I can review it.

A SUMMER MESSENGER.

You poor, weak, trembling little breeze,
   That scarce can move my papers,
Are you the lusty wind of March
   That played such merry capers ?

You blew my hat across the street,
   And whistled while I chased it,—
The while a laughing crowd stood by
   To see if I outpaced it.

To-day you come so meek and mild—
   As if you feared my anger ;
Or more, perhaps, as if you, too,
   Had caught our Summer languor.

Come, little breeze, you need a change ;
   I 'll send you in this letter
To help a dear girl, whom I know,
   Grow stronger, too, and better.

Return, then, to your mountain home,
   Grow strong again and sprightly ;
And when her cheeks are flushed with heat,
   Be sure and fan them lightly.

Blow sweet scents from your mountain pines
   Between her half-closed shutters,—
You 'll be repaid, if her brown hair
   Entwines you when it flutters.

But, first, when she shall break the seal,
   And set you free around her,
Ask her if all the thoughts of love
   I 've sent to her have found her.

And if, perchance, you see her blush,
   Tell her how much I miss her ;
And if she says she 's glad—well, yes,
   Since *I* can't, *you* may kiss her.

AN IMPOSSIBLE GIRL.

ONCE on a time there lived a maid
Who never was of mice afraid,
A perfect game of whist she played,—
    This maid entrancing.
Of gowns and styles she never talked,
Attempts to compliment she balked,
For exercise she only walked—
    She hated dancing.

She wore no loud, queer-colored glove,
She never yet had been in love,
Her bureau held no picture of
    The latest actor ;
And, furthermore, she never went
To matinées, nor ever spent
Her change for soda ; roses sent
    Could not attract her.

Of slang she never used a word,
Of flirting she had never heard,
Society—it seems absurd—
    She did not care for.

At gay resorts, where men were not,
She never seemed to care a jot,—
Until the mothers wondered what
    The girl was there for.

No one will know from whence she came;
She left no record but her fame;
Not even can we learn her name
    Or what her station.
When did she live? How did she die?
She lived in fancy. Tis a lie.
I 've only tried to practise my
    Imagination.

2

EASTER.

A LONG farewell to the cloth called "sack,"
To fasting and service and prayers, alack,
    And ashes for Beauty's adorning ;
For, oh, what visions, in bonnet and gown,
With eyes that shine as though never a frown
Had marred their brightness, will storm the town,
    With the light of the Easter morning !

When the bells that peal so loud and deep
Wake Mephistopheles out of the sleep
    That for forty days has claimed him,
His smiling friends will greet him again,—
The maids and the matrons, youths and men,—
As warmly as though there was no time when
    They had neither known nor named him.

For all of the churches, "low" and "high,"
Have done their part, and tis now good-bye
    To missal and hymn and sermon.
For forty days have they had their place,
And society, filled with the Lenten grace,
Is turning now with a smiling face
    To theatre, ball, and german.

And surely the comfort is great to some,
To feel that by simply abstaining from
    " The world, the flesh, and the devil,"
For forty days, they have all the year
Except that forty, without a fear,
To enjoy themselves till they leave this sphere,
    In a frolic of fun and revel.

And though, of course, to be truly good
Is what we strive for, and ever should,
    There 's another excellent reason
Why youth to observe it is always bent,
For many engagements are made in Lent,
And, moreover, it seems a time that 's meant
    To prepare for the Summer season.

This year of 1894, **St. Valentine's** the date,

Now this Indenture Witnesseth:

That, of my whole estate,
To her I love the best I give, **To have and hold**
forever,
In full fee simple absolute, the **True Love** of the
giver.
But lest the grantee in this deed should ever wish to
alienate
To others, from herself, the whole or any part of this
estate,
Unless she first shall have obtained from the said
grantor his permission,
And do the same with his consent,

20

𝕹𝖔𝖜, 𝕿𝖍𝖊𝖗𝖊𝖋𝖔𝖗𝖊,

this express 𝕮𝖔𝖓𝖉𝖎𝖙𝖎𝖔𝖓

Is unto this said gift attached, That if she any part of this

Conveyed estate, however small, shall give away, she owes a 𝕶𝖎𝖘𝖘

To the said grantor in this deed, unless the said grantor relents,

𝕭𝖚𝖙 *if he doth not he may claim the penalty for each offence.*

And the said grantor herein named, in testimony of his love,

Has set hereto his hand and seal, the day and year first named above.

James G. Burnett

PHOTOGRAPHS.

THAT picture ?   A relic of summer.
  I met her at—yes, Mt. Desert,
And thought her just short of an angel :
  She proved to be only a flirt.

That 's Nellie.   Oh, don't you remember
  The night of the Charity Ball,
Where she was the fairest of any,
  Her laughter the lightest of all ?

Say, Harry, there 's one that 's familiar ;
  And this one.   Yes, two of a kind.
I know I was " pretty well smitten "—
  No wonder they say Love is blind.

There 's Edith—I quite had forgotten
  Her picture was in among those.
You knew her—the belle of the season,
  And I was but one of her beaux.

And here 's one—you 'll laugh when you see it—
  A tintype we got at the shore—
The girls we met down at the races,
  The day that we played Salvator.

There 's Jessie, and Kittie, and Carrie—
  Dear girls, I was fond of all three :
But each of them married some fellow
  Who met her the first time through me.

This evening I 'm looking them over,
  These pictures of girls I have known ;
And Memory 's reaping a harvest
  From hours of pleasure I 've sown.

Touch gently this last one, old fellow,—
  I prize it all others above :
For they were but fancies and follies,
  But this is the girl that I love.

TO A VERY YOUNG LADY.

Pray tell me, Margery, why it is
  That you, who are so fair,
And so complete in other ways,
  Should not have any hair.

Do you not know tis hard to write—
  If such they may be called,—
Love songs and sonnets to a girl
  Who 's very nearly bald ?

I wonder that a little hair
  Should seem so far beneath
The notice even of a girl
  Who does not care for teeth ;

For pretty hair and teeth help out
  A poet's halting rhyme,
And no one can write clever songs
  To blue eyes all the time.

But when some eighteen Summers fair
   Those added charms shall bring,
You 'll be surprised, and maybe pleased,
   With all the songs I 'll sing.

FEBRUARY FOURTEENTH.

To send a heart, as others do,
   I know is fitting at this season ;
And I would gladly send one too,
   Except for one important reason.

For even if I surely knew
   That if I did I should repent it,
I would to-day send mine to you,
   If I had not—already sent it.

INDECISION.

WERE Julia not so kindly sweet,
   And Lena sweetly kind ;
If either's charms were less complete,
   Or I to one were blind,—

Ah, then to part and say good-bye
   Would be but little more,
And give no other pang, than I
   Have often felt before.

But both are witty, bright, and true,
   And winning, frank, and fair.
Would that my fickle heart I knew,
   And which was dearer there.

THE DEBUTANTE.

I BLUSH if I look in the mirror ;
  I sigh while I do up my hair ;
Whenever I 'm told I am pretty,
  I wonder if some one will care.

I start if he speaks to me quickly,
  I tremble at taking his hand,
While he only murmurs, " Good evening.
  Why is it men can't understand ?

I wish I could tell if he liked me ;
  He 's exactly the same to us all :
To-night he took me to the German—
  He 'll take Belle to the Masquerade Ball.

Oh, I hope he don't know that I like him ;
  I fear that I must have seemed bold
When I said, " I am *so glad* to see you " ;
  Well, I 'm sure I don't want to seem cold.

27

How royally handsome, this evening,
  He looked in the midst of those men ;
The rest were but shadows beside him.
  Oh, I wish I could hear him again

Say he hoped that I " was n't too tired,"
  As the waltz's last strains died away.
Oh, mercy ! What nonsense I 'm thinking !
  If I told Mamma, what would she say ?

I thought he would feel my hand tremble,
  When he offered to button my glove.
Oh, I know that he does n't care for me.
  Heigh-ho ! I 'm afraid I 'm in love.

A GAME OF WHIST.

ETHEL : Whose deal ? Mine ? I declare ! I thought
 I dealt before.

Now, (*dealing to her partner*) Tom, we really must make
 more.

Diamonds are trumps, and—

    MAY : Whose lead ?

      DICK (*mildly*) : Yours, Miss May.

MAY : Oh, of course. How stupid ! Yes. *I* don't
 know what to play.

But (*throws an ace*) we 're sure of *one*. What ! must I
 play again ?

Well (*leads another*)—

    ETHEL : I do like to play with men !

They always keep so quiet and—

     MAY : That 's what I like, too.

You can't play whist and talk. At least I can't. (*To
Dick*) Can you ?

DICK (*smiling*) : Oh, yes ; pretty well. (*Aside*) Well,
 I 'm a chump

If I play whist with girls again.

29

MAY : What ! my play ? What 's trump ?

TOM : Diamonds.

DICK : Clubs led, Miss May.

MAY : Well, if that 's the case
I think I 'll trump it.

ETHEL : May, that was your partner's ace.

MAY : Never mind ; we got the trick. (*To Dick*) You 're
in the dumps
Because I took it.

DICK : Your play.

MAY : Mine ? Oh, yes. What 's trumps ?

ETHEL : Now, we must make the odd. We really must,
indeed.
My play ? Well, there !

TOM (*sadly*) : That was our opponent's lead.

ETHEL : I thought *you* led it. Well, it does n't matter.
Say,
What *are* the trumps ?

TOM : Diamonds.

DICK : You took that trick, Miss May.

MAY : Did I ? Oh, yes. Well, let 's see--I 'll play *that*
then. (*Dick starts*)
Why, what 's the matter—is that wrong ?

DICK (*grimly*) : Tom trumps hearts.

TOM (*leading diamonds*) : " When in doubt——"

ETHEL : My play again ?

MAY : What *are* trumps ?

DICK : Diamonds.

MAY : Oh, yes. What ails you men ? Don't you think whist is fun ? I do. Why, you look just as glum.

DICK (*feebly*) : Do I ?

TOM (*aside*) : I wish these girls were dumb.

DICK : We think this is fine.

TOM : Yes, the pleasure is intense. We 've had a most delightful time, I 'm sure.

DICK : Just immense !

MAY : *We 've* enjoyed it.

ETHEL : Yes ; we do so like to play A scientific game of whist—with men, too—don't we, May ?

A THWARTED AMBITION.

I would I were a " funny man,"
    But Fate has been unkind ;
I have no stock in trade of jokes
    Such as they seem to find.

My baby does not cry at night ;
    My gas bills are not large ;
The plumber makes, I must admit,
    A reasonable charge.

My cook is all that I could wish ;
    And hash I never saw ;
A gentler woman does not live
    Than is my mother-in-law.

My coat has never carried home
    A hair from some stray curl ;
I never knew a hotel clerk,
    Nor had a " Summer girl."

Typewriters do not bother me—
  My own is quick and neat ;
The only Western girl I knew
  Had very dainty feet.

The theatre hats I 've sat behind
  Were of a modest height ;
The bathing dresses I have seen
  Were never " out of sight."

The chorus girls I 've known were young ;
  The choirs I 've heard could sing ;
I sometimes even like to read
  A dainty " Ode to Spring."

And so, although I 'd like to be
  One of those funny folks,
I have to give it up, because
  Where could I get my jokes ?

3

A TALE OF THE RACES.

He could tell you all the horses
That had run at all the courses,
When they ever held a meeting,
  Since the racing year began.
And not only could he tell you
All their names, but he could—well, you
See he made their form a study—
  Say exactly *how* they ran.

For he knew which horse was leading
At each quarter, and their breeding,
With the time for every quarter,
  And the horse that won the race.
He knew which had "sulked" or faltered,
And just how it would have altered
Their positions at the finish
  Had the favorite made the pace.

He knew records to a second,
Who had made them, and had reckoned
Just what other horse could do it,
  When the track was fast or slow.

34

He remembered, too, the betting,
And the jockeys, not forgetting
To note specially the distance
   Every one of them could go.

So you see, in half a minute
He knew just what horse could win it,
.Whether at a mile or over,
   Or a short six-furlong dash.
Then he never hesitated,
Not a single instant waited,
But he backed them in the betting
   For a goodly pile of cash.

As a " plunger " he was noted,
And his " tips " were often quoted ;
Be it fair or stormy weather,
   He was always at the track.
He came always, too, with money,
But, although—tis very funny—
He could tell so much about them,
   He was always walking back.

TWILIGHT FANCIES.

At twilight, floating fancies swarm,
　In circling flights, about my head,—
All bright with roseate, radiant thoughts,
　And words that angels might have said.

But when I try to hold them fast,
　As I have done so many times,
I find them far too light and free
　To ever catch and cage in rhymes.

As moths about a shining light,
　Or honeysuckle, gleam and whirr,
The brightest-colored fancies float
　About my sweetest thoughts of her ;

Like moths, one moment softly rest,
　But, as I touch them with my pen,
Like them they spread their downy wings,
　And float off into space again.

But if some brilliant moth be caught,—
　The brightest of those fluttering things,—
It shows, in morning's light, without
　One ray of color on its wings.

And so my brightest fancies fade,
　My fairest thoughts I always miss,
And find my memory holding fast
　To some dull gray one—such as this.

FAITH.

WE know not God in all His wondrous might,
　Yet feel each day His love and watchful care.
With naked eyes we may not view the light
　Of noonday sun, and yet the sun is there.

HER NOTE.

Her dainty envelope is square—
I think, the while its seal I tear,
So like herself, both sweet and fair ;
The note inside it, too, I 'll swear,
        Light and diverting.

What though her heart be free from care,
And blue her eyes and soft her hair,
Her voice like Southern breezes rare—
There 's not one touch of feeling there :
        She 's only flirting.

SOLILOQUIES.

HIS DOCTOR.

He 's surely failing very fast ;
   He 's really very ill.
I fear he 'll not much longer last—
   I must prepare my bill.

HIS LAWYER.

Poor fellow, dying.   Such is fate.
   Well, that will bring to me
The settling up of his estate—
   Which means a rousing fee.

HIS WIFE.

Such trials come to all in life,
   And have to be endured.
Of course tis harder for a wife—
   But then, he is insured.

39

THE UNDERTAKER.

He 's surely dying very slow.
  His funeral won't be grand,
But ought to be a good thing, though—
  I wonder what they 'll stand.

THE PATIENT.

I cling not to my failing life,
  Though grief its loss attends
In parting from my loving wife
  And my unselfish friends

NOT A BOSTON GIRL.

I SEAL the letter, write her name—
  Tis very dear to me,—
And then I add unto the same,
  Two letters—M and D.

I see you smile in quick disdain ;
  You think of glasses, too,
And little curls. Tis very plain
  What "M.D." means to you.

But she is neither stern nor cold,
  As you perhaps may think.
She 's young and fair, not grim and old ;
  , Nor does she scatter ink

On notes of lessons that are said
  Before a learnéd class ;
And from her dainty lips of red
  No long orations pass.

The only treatises she reads
  Are letters that I write ;
The only lectures that she heeds
  Are those that I indite.

You wonder how it all may be,
  And do not understand ?
She lives in Baltimore.   Md.
  Means, simply,—Maryland.

THE RIGHT PLACE.

HE had been to the mountains, and down by the sea,
  All the Summer—for health was his quest ;
And when he returned to his home, tired out,
And again with its comforts was circled about,
  He said, "Well, it was all for the best ;
This Summer is wasted, and I am a wreck,
But next year will find me restored and on deck,
  For I 'll stay in the city, and rest."

UP TO DATE.

"WHERE are you going, my pretty maid?"
"I 'm going to Dakota, sir," she said.

"May I go with you, my pretty maid?"
"Do you wish a divorce, too, sir?" she said.

"What is your fortune, my pretty maid?"
"My alimony, sir," she said.

"Then I can't marry you, my pretty maid."
"I 'm already engaged, kind sir," she said.

JUDGE AND JESTER.

WHEN most by Reason I am sought,
 With graver themes, ofttimes
My foolish Fancy turns to naught,
 And runs to making rhymes :

Like to that judge of quaint renown,—
 He who, tradition tells,
Light-hearted, doffed his wig and gown,
 To wear the cap and bells.

But when from care I turn away,
 To greet my smiling Wit,
My mind is like a court that day,
 Where Thought and Wisdom sit.

Would that my Fancy did not grudge
 To own some honest rule,
And knew when best to act the judge,
 And when to play the fool.

A PROVERBIAL PLEA.

If "kissing goes by favor," as
  The wise folk all agree,
Oh, why, my pretty maid, wilt thou
  Not sometimes favor me?

If "pity is akin to love,"
  And many say it be,
I pray thee, tender-hearted girl,
  A little pity me.

And if "faint heart ne'er won" a maid,
  I pledge my word to thee,
No man e'er wore a bolder heart
  Than I will bear in me.

If "absence makes the heart grow fond,"
  I 'll cross the land and sea,
And dwell in hope that, far away,
  Thou wilt grow fond of me.

45

But if " Love goes where it is sent,"
  Oh, set young Cupid free,
And make him thy swift messenger
  To bear thy love to me.

If " love me little, love me long "
  Will move thee, hear my plea—
Howe'er so little, so tis long,
  Will be enough for me.

UNVALUED.

A BETTER impulse, from the violets tost,
  Came to the sodden man upon the grass :
He never knew the sense of something lost,
  Though he had let it pass.

MY TYPEWRITER.

WHENE'ER I see her pretty face,
  Low o'er the key-board bending,
And watch her winning, girlish grace
  To this old office lending
Unwonted gleams of sunny light,
  I can't think, I declare,
That she 's the girl with whom I fight
  Sometimes, and almost swear.

And as I watch her fingers pink
  Fast flying o'er the keys,
Half tenderly I sit and think
  Of what my fancy sees.
And at the end of every day,
  When she, with whom I 've battled,
Has gone, to her machine I say :
  " No wonder you get rattled ! "

AN IDEAL.

IF I had the facile pencil
Of a Gibson or a Wenzell,
I would draw a girl beside whom
  Every other girl should fade.
For within my mind's recesses,
Fairer than your wildest guesses,
I have long and fondly cherished
  The one fair, ideal maid.

She should be as bright and witty,
And as natty, arch, and pretty,
As the fairest and the brightest
  That was ever seen in life.
She should be no more than human
Not an angel, but a woman,
And that woman of all others
  That a man would call his wife.

Fairer yet than outward seeming
Is the soul of which I 'm dreaming ;
And the graces of her spirit,
  All that 's sweet and pure and good,

All that Love and Truth can teach her,
Shine through every radiant feature.—
Though I never hope to meet her,
    I would know her if I should.

A SUGGESTION.

THE doctors now are in distress
    Because of the objection,
Made by the people and the press,
    To wholesale vivisection.

But it would lose, I much suspect,
    A host of the objectors,
If Science would but vivisect
    Some of the vivisectors.

A TOAST.

In all the love songs everywhere,
   Tis strange and yet tis true
That all the girls have golden hair,
   Their eyes are always blue.

But though the tender eyes of blue
   Inspire so many rhymes,
The brown-eyed girls have lovers too,
   And claim a song sometimes.

As for my heart,—soft, light-brown hair,
   And eyes of deeper shade,
Have left a tenderer impress there
   Than blue eyes ever made.

And while the blue-eyed maidens live
   In other poets' lays,
A modest verse or two I 'll give
   To brown-eyed maidens' praise.

And may the songs we each shall write
   The pleasure to us bring
Of finding favor in the sight
   Of her whose charms we sing.

So, brothers of the pen, to you
   I drink this bumper down :
Long may you write to eyes of blue,
   And I to eyes of brown !

A GOOD SHOT.

" DEATH loves a shining mark."   If so
    Tis rather strange
He does not make the "baldhead row "
    His rifle - range.

A NOBLE BOY.

A FATHER spake unto his son,
  The youth drew nigh to hear :
"My boy, take this small pitcher out
  And have it filled with beer."

Then calmly said the noble boy,
  "My father, you may break
Your wrath upon me, but for beer
  That pitcher I 'll not take."

"Ah, Heaven !" cried the stricken man,
  "This, from my child, is rough."
"Why, father," quickly cried the lad,
  "It does n't hold enough."

PIKE'S PEAK.

THIS rugged mountain, æons old,
 For ages all untrod,
Has raised its head since time began,
 A monument to God.

A thousand thousand Summer suns,
 In all their wondrous might,
Have rested there, but failed to melt
 The giant's crown of white.

Before that mighty altar men
 With reverent hearts have bowed,
And sought, with awe-struck gaze, to pierce
 The summit's drifting cloud.

Beneath the moonbeams' silver touch
 It rises grim and gray.—
The same light floods your room to-night
 Two thousand miles away.

Two thousand miles !   A little space
　　When hearts are warm and true,—
For while I watch Pike's Peak to-night
　　My thoughts are all with you.

IN OTHER DAYS.

In other days the trees were brighter green ;
　　In other days the sky was deeper blue ;
In other days life's fairest joys were seen,
　　Because of you.

In other days you loved me, so you said ;
　　In other days I thought you pure and true :
And now, alas, I would that I were dead,
　　Because of you !

FANCIE FREE.

Nott to any Mayde alone
Long allegeance will I own.
  Juste as soone
    Her Squier
Would I reste content to be.
I will follow Minstralcie,
And for alle who smile on Me
  Will I tune
    My Lyre.

On brown Eyes & Eyes of blewe,
Black & gray & everie hewe,
  Many sighes
    I 've wasted.
Beauty's Charmes I 've bowed before,
Beauty's Lippes I still adore,
And thaire Swetes, lyke many more,
  Being wys,
    I 've tasted.

In my Memorie, Wurd & Song,
Daies yt. never were too long
　　　Art enrolled.
　　　　　Ingraven
On my Harte are many Names,
Gentyl Damsels, stately Dames,
Faces sette in daintie Frames,
　　　Tresses gold
　　　　　And raven

Surely Fate is kynde to Me !
Thoughe admiring, Fancie free
　　　Doth She let
　　　　　Me tarry.
To ye sette of Youthe's bright Sunne
May I love as I 've begon,
Alle I meet, nor thynke there 's one
　　　Better yet,
　　　　　And marry.

"ACCEPTED."

It happened one day that a poet whose rhymes
    Very seldom appeared in the press—
So seldom, poor fellow, between you and me,
    That they could n't appear any less—

Remarked to his wife, when he kissed her good-bye,
    As he usually did, at the door,
" Our money is gone, and I really don't know
    How on earth, dear, to get any more.

" The market is dull, and I can't sell a thing,
    Though of excellent rhymes I 've no lack,
And how dull it is you may know when I say
    That they send even dialect back."

His wife only smiled,—she 'd a dear little smile
    That would brighten and bless any life,
And a heart that by Nature was surely designed
    To belong to a poor poet's wife.

That evening, disheartened, he came to his home,
  And his wife met him right at the door,
A big roll of bank notes held close in her hand—
  Oh, a couple of hundred or more.

" Your poems," she cried, " I have sold every one !"
  (And the poor fellow's heart gave a bound).
" Yes, is n't it lovely ?   I sold them—just think !—
  To a junk man, at one cent a pound."

TEXAS.

In days like this my life goes by—
A Summer sun, a cloudless sky,
A stretch of prairie brown and bare,
And deathless silence everywhere.

A REVERIE.

LET me read the songs I sung,
  Ne'er the moments timing,
When my pen and I were young
  In the art of rhyming.
When, I wonder, did I write
  Rhymes as soft as this is ?—

" Since that happy, fateful night
    I have felt your kisses.
  Fancy brings that moment back "—

Cæsar !   I was loony.
That is what my nephew Jack
  Designates as " spoony."
Did I not write something good ?—

" MARY.

" Your caresses "—

Well, I used to think I could.
  Here is one I guess is
Somewhat better than the rest ;

But this " Toast to Hebe "
Hardly can be called the best.
Here are

" LINES TO PHŒBE.

" Phœbe's face is sweet and fair,"—

That, at least, was truthful.

" Phœbe's smile would banish care "—

Yes, when I was youthful !
Since that time I 've wiser grown,
And a trifle older ;
Cupid leaves me quite alone—
Then the rogue was bolder.
Once he hovered o'er my pen
Like a bee 'round honey ;
For I wrote him verses then—
Now I write for money.

NOT FOR ME.

I SEE the love-light shining fair,
  Half hid, within her eyes,
And wonder if perchance she 'd care
  To know I heard her sighs.

I sigh, myself, and turn away ;
  No longer may I see.
The love-light shining there to-day
  Will never shine for me.

BEREAVEMENT.

I LOVED him as we only love one friend.
Through life we walked, in all things side by side.
He shared with all men both their joy and care ;
      ´   And, living so, he died :
Like common mortals, met the common end.
The world has lost a man it ill could spare ;
      And I have lost a friend.

LOST OPPORTUNITIES.

When I was a tiny lad,
  A very little fellow,
Wore a kilted skirt of plaid
  And curls of shining yellow,—

Then I thought that little girls
  Were very far below me ;
But I 've lost my yellow curls,
  And now you would n't know me.

Then I used to scorn the kiss
  They sometimes freely offered ;
Now, alas ! such earthly bliss
  Is never to me proffered.

Would that I again might wear
  Those shining curls of yellow !
Girls would find me now, I 'll swear,
  A wiser sort of fellow.

A SOUTHERN GIRL.

HER eyes
  Would match her Southern skies,
    That all their beauty lend her ;
Their light,
  Like stars of Southern night,
    Is soft and clear and tender.

Bright pearls,
  The gems of Southern girls,
    Her winning smile discloses ;
Her cheeks,
  When admiration speaks,
    Wear only Southern roses.

Her laugh,
  As light as wine or chaff,
    Breaks clear, at witty sallies,
As brooks
  Run bubbling through the nooks
    Of all her Southern valleys.

Her voice,
  By nature and by choice,
    E'en those who know her slightest
Will find
  As soft as Southern wind
    When Southern winds are lightest.

Such youth,
  With all its charms, forsooth,—
    Alas, too well I know it !—
Will claim
  A song of love and fame,
    Sung by some Southern poet.

But she,
  In future years, maybe,
    These verses will discover,—
Sometime
  May read this little rhyme
    Sung by a Northern lover.

TO J. H. M.

WHAT friendly goddess did to you
  This wondrous gift impart ?
So perfect that we hesitate
  To call it only art !

You paint an evening scene so we
  May feel its subtle hush ;
A wave, as though that wave itself
  Had broken from your brush.

If you yourself are strong as are
  The waves you love so much,
And if your heart be true and light
  As is your fingers' touch,

To know you well would make more smooth
  Rough ways we all have trod :
A man so near to Nature must
  Live very near to God.

5

HER THOUGHTS.

"A penny for your thoughts," he said,
And saucily she raised her head
    To meet his searching eyes ;
She laughed, and blushed a vivid red,
Then shyly, "Oh, how stupid, Fred,
    A man is, when he tries.

" For they are not, so I 've been taught,
Such things as can be sold or bought ;
    And, oh, you foolish Freddy—
You did n't know it ? Well, you ought,—
That I have not a single thought
    That is not yours already."

A LEGEND OF LOVE.

MANY years ago a Princess
   Lived within a castle old,
With a stern, sad King, her father,
   Of whom many tales were told,—
Told by gray-haired men and women,
   With a trembling voice and tongue,
Who recalled the happy hours
   When the aged King was young.

How he loved a foreign Princess
   Of a sweet and gentle mien,
And had brought her home in triumph,
   There to reign his people's Queen ;
How the castle walls resounded
   With the joy her presence brought
And the King, to please her fancy,
   Every day new pleasures sought.

How he grew the more enraptured
   With her graces pure and sweet,
And was less her lord and sovereign
   Than a vassal at her feet :

Told, with husky voice, and sadly,
　　How the common people cried—
For they all had known and loved her—
　　When the gentle Princess died.

How the King grew stern and altered,
　　Cursed the God who reigned above,
Closed his heart to human kindness,
　　And his castle gates to love.
But the young Queen left a daughter,
　　And, in memory of his wife,
All his shattered hopes and feelings
　　Centred 'round this daughter's life.

And the cherished little Princess
　　Grew to beauty sweet and rare,
With her mother's gentle nature,
　　And her crown of golden hair.
All her life was passed from childhood
　　In her father's oaken halls,
And she never knew that people
　　Lived beyond his castle walls,

Till one day was heard a bugle,—
　　Came a knocking at the gate,
From a young and knightly stranger
　　Who had halted there in state.

Went the old King forth to greet him,
   With a frown upon his face,
But the young knight, smiling, met him
   With a frank and courtly grace ;

Asked a lodging till the morrow,
   Was a pilgrim in the land,
Craved his pardon for intruding,
   Knelt and kissed his withered hand.
So the youthful traveller tarried ;
   And when evening shadows came,
Lo, the startled King with sorrow
   Heard his guest's unwelcome name.

Once more Love had gained an entrance
   To his castle strong and grim,
And his sweet young voice rang clearly
   In the sacred evening hymn.
And the old man, sad and silent,
   Heard the lordly stranger sing,
Till a thrill of tender passion
   Swept the sorrow-broken King.

And the young knight found a welcome ;
   And the days passed into weeks,—
Till the Princess told her secret
   In the blushes on her cheeks.

So it was Love conquered Sorrow,
  And ascended to the throne,
Where he ruled the grand old castle
  With a glory all his own.

.   .   .   .   .   .

Once again the King was happy,—
  And with misty eyes he smiled,
As he told her mother's story
  To his daughter's little child.

WHY SONGS ARE SUNG.

Tis not for honors he may win
  The poet's songs are sung ;
Tis not for these he lets us in
  To worlds he lives among.

No bay nor laurel would he wear ;
  But that for which he longs
Is only that some one, somewhere,
  May learn to love his songs.

LIMITATION.

.We know not of the other life.
  Why hope or fear ?
Enough that this is pain and strife,
  And we are here.

OUR GIRLS.

I SING a song for modern girls,
   Against those girls of old
Whose wondrous charms of face and mind
   In many a song are told.

Sweet Peggy, who, on market day,
   Set Samuel Lover singing,
So that he sent her praise in rhyme
   Down all the century ringing,

Was not, within her low-backed car,
   A fairer sight, I trow,
Than many a maid who drives about
   Within a dog-cart, now.

The girl you left behind you, too,
   Ye fifers and ye drummers,
Was not, I ween, a dearer girl,
   Then we 've left, many Summers.

And I am sure that little Ray,
  Who dances in the ballet,
Is just as sweet, and loved as much,
    As Sally in Our Alley.

Why, even dear Tom Moore, who wrote,
  With many loving sighs,
Of " Fanny's hands," and " Jenny's lips,"
  And " Lesbia's beaming eyes,"

Would, I am sure, agree with me
  If he had lived to-day,
And sigh for words to sing the praise
  Of Molly, Maud, or May.

THE RIVAL MINSTRELS.

HAROUN AL RASCHID loved his harem's maids ;
He loved his gardens, with their winding shades ;
He loved to watch his crystal fountains play ;
He loved his horses, and his courtiers gay :
He loved all royal sports that please a king,
But most he loved to hear his minstrels sing.

And so it happened that his fame had brought
Two rival singers who his favor sought.
Who pleased him best, full well each minstrel knew,
Would be proclaimed the greater of the two.
So well they pleased him that they found him loath
To choose between them, for he loved them both.

" Let all the nation judge," at length said he ;
" Who pleases best my people pleases me."
Through all the land the rival poets sung,
Their names and music were on every tongue,
Until at length they never reached a door
Where Fame had not sung all their songs before.

Ben Olaf sang of deeds the Caliph wrought,
And all the splendors that his riches brought ;
The mighty warriors every nation boasts,
And armies vanquished by the Prophet's hosts ;
How Islam's valor was beloved, and feared :
And when he finished, listening thousands cheered.

Mustapha's songs were all of simpler things :
Forgotten was the pride of earthly kings.
He sang to them of home, and truth, and love ;
How Allah watched his children from above.
Close to their hearts the poet's music crept,
And when he finished, all the people wept.

For though Ben Olaf charmed them with his arts,
It was Mustapha's songs that reached their hearts.

ENCOURAGEMENT.

"If I were you I would not flirt
   With every girl I knew,"
Once said a little maiden pert.
   Quoth I, " What would you do,

" If you and I could change our place,
   (Suppose such things could be)
And while I gained your girlish grace,
   You were transformed to me ? "

Then did this little maiden cry,
   " You ask what I would do
If you were in my place ? Why, I
   Would only flirt with you ! "

THE ANGEL SONG.

THERE 's an old, sweet song that the angels sing,
  That we all have heard when we still were young,
And would hear it now with a throbbing heart— ·
  Tis the evening song that our mothers sung.

How it hushed our sorrows and childish griefs,—
  Such little griefs, but they brought their tears :
And the echo of that sweet evening song
  Brings me peace even now, after all these years.

As it soothed my troubles and strifes with boys,
  As I lay on her bosom and heard it then,
So it echoes over the chasm of years,
  And strengthens me now in the war with men.

Borne down with a burden of grief and care,
  And weary of ceaseless struggle and strife,
Under the ban of my merciless fate
  I have raged and raved at the curse of life—

When, out of the silence, that dear old song,
  That I 'll not forget in an age of time,
Comes sweet to my ear with the same low tune,
  Goes straight to my heart with the well-known rhyme.

And so tis a fancy I sometimes have,
  A conceit that is strange, and it may be wrong,
That the song I heard in my childhood days
  Comes back to me now as an angel's song.

IN LOVE'S DOMAIN.

In Love's domain, while lasts the day,
    How swift Time's flight.
In Love's domain, when shines the sun,
  · How warm and bright.
    But oh, the night !

THE SUMMER GIRL.

OH, the Summer now is ended,
  And from mountain, lake and shore,
Cityward her way is wended
  By the Summer Girl once more.

All the color of the roses
  In her cheeks she brings to town,
And the greatest of her woes is
  That her neck and arms are brown.

When again we chance to meet her,
  Clad in dainty robes of fur,
We are lucky when we greet her
  If we get a smile from her.

For no charm has faded from her
  In the city's giddy whirl,
And as fondly as the Summer
  Do we love the Winter Girl.

THE POET.

He sang too near to Nature's tones
  To please the critic's art ;
His songs were music from his soul,
  The echoes of his heart.

He could not train his thoughts to flow
  Like water serving mills ;
They ran and leapt with foaming strength,
  As run the mountain rills.

They shone as shines a flaring torch
  Beside a well-trimmed flame ;
The people loved to read his songs,
  And smiled to speak his name,—

Not they who measure music's voice
  By rhythmic rule, but those
Who find a new and sweet delight
  Where every violet grows.

And when the clarion voice was stilled,
    And quenched the heart of flame,
The critics learned at last how great
    Had been the poet's fame.

HOPE.

WHEN in the West I see the dying sun
    Sink out of sight,
I know that when the coming night is done
    There will be light.

And when with sorrow and with earthly care
    I am oppressed,
I think with peace of life's to-morrow, where
    There will be rest.

6

ELLEN'S PRAYER-BOOK.

No volume bound in red and gold,
Of tales of warriors brave and bold,
No dearly valued, worn and old,
    Time-stained edition
Of some Greek Bible, quaint and rare,
Or rhymes in praise of ladies fair,
But just a little Book of Prayer,
    And this its mission :

To rest each week in Ellen's hands,
As prettily devout she stands
And reads her prayers and God's commands
    From out its covers ;
And when her eyes demurely fall
To read of Peter or of Paul,
It wins an envious glance from all
    Of Ellen's lovers.

Ah, in your trust and sweet belief
In God and truth, be life too brief
To set one rugged line of grief
    On your fair brow ;

May He to whom you chant these psalms
Guard you through life from all its harms,
And meet you with His outstretched arms,
  As pure as now.

WHITHER.

THE night is dark and stormy
  On life's unsettled sea,
But clear and bright the morning
  When sets the tide to thee.

Backward and forward drifting
  My ship forever goes,
And if it reach the harbor,
  Alas, God only knows !

A PASSING FANCY.

I sit alone to-night, and in the grate
  I watch the dying flame flash up and gleam
An instant through the dark.   Tis growing late,
  And still in silence do I sit and dream.

The fancies that I see within its light
  Are sometimes like its ashes—cold and dark ;
Another moment flashing up as bright
  As if in keeping with its brightest spark.

But why should I sit sadly here to-night ?
  Others are fair, if one but thinks they are.
That last red coal will make a splendid light,
  And—ah, by Jove, but that 's a good cigar !

HER FACE.

In dreams I see it, sweet and fair,
Within a frame of soft brown hair,
That sometimes in rebellion flies
Across a pair of starry eyes.
And such a soft, delicious shade
Of color has this little maid—
A bright and pure and radiant hue,
As though her soul were shining through.

If this were all, we still might dare
To hope we could escape the snare
That Cupid weaves and deftly throws
About us, with such charms as those.
But to destroy one ling'ring chance
We might have had, to meet her glance
And not be taken captive quite,
Upon her cheeks of rosy light
Twin dimples play at hide and seek,
Whene'er she dares to smile or speak.

I think some angel in her room
Has seen a tear shine through the gloom,
Upon her cheeks, when she has wept,
And lightly kissed them while she slept.
Since then, her smile, with heavenly grace,
Shows where the angel touched her face.

THE EVENING STAR.

THE evening star looks in.
    What finds he here to see?
Naught in this room hath been
    Except my thoughts and me.

My thoughts are black as jet;
    He shines serenely bright.
My star of hope has set;
    He 's rising for the night.

MY LADY DISDAIN.

THINK thou not, fair maid, that scorn
   Brings me closer yet unto thee,
Or that I shall sigh forlorn
   That another comes to woo thee.

If thou smile on all who come,
   Do not also smile on me ;
If to me thy lips are dumb,
   Mine are also dumb to thee.

One who cares for many knights
   May not count me in her train.
Faith that knows so many plights
   Is a faith that I disdain.

If my love thou choose to slight,
   I have naught of love to give ;
And my heart shall still be light
   As thy fancy, while I live.

AT THE TELEPHONE.

HELLO! Say, Central! Hello, there ;
　　Give me three forty-four.
Yes, Thirty-eighth. No time to spare—
　　I 've just one minute more.
What 's that? "A hurry"? Yes, of course.—
　　"Don't shout so any more "?
I 'll keep on shouting till I 'm hoarse,
　　Or get three forty-four.

　　·　　·　　·　　·　　·　　·

No, they 're *not* " busy "—they can't be ;
　　I tell you I live there.—
What 's that you say ?—You don't ? We 'll see ;
　　Perhaps I 'll *make* you care.

　　·　　·　　·　　·　　·　　·

Say, Central, won't you hurry ? Say,
　　Please get that for me soon ;
I want to talk to them to-day—
　　Not in next May or June.

　　·　　·　　·　　·　　·　　·

Come, get a move on ; you 're too slow.—
   Who 's " funny " ?   Just one more
Impertinence like that, and—Oh !
   Is that three forty-four ?
Is that you, Daisy ?—Can't you hear ?—
   Now, wait, I 'll say it slow.—
Yes, Jack, *me*—JACK—now listen, dear :—
   Say, Daisy, do you know—
Don't cut us off, I tell you—where
   (George ! how these wires sing !)
My papers are ?—I *did n't* swear.
   (*Great Cæsar !*   D—n this thing !)

.   .   .   .   .   .

Look on the hat-rack in the hall—
   (Connection 's bad, of course—
It always *is.*—*Confound* it all !)—
   No, dear, I am *not* cross.—
Yes, on the hat-rack.—All right, dear,
   I 'll wait.—Yes, my court docket.—
I 'll *wait*, I say.   .   .   .
           Can't find it ?—Here,
   Great Scott !   It 's in my pocket !

PERPLEXING.

" MISTRESS Mary, quite contrary,"
    Sang a poet long ago,—
Though just why he mentioned Mary
    Is what I should like to know.

Why distinguish Mistress Mary
    From her sisters everywhere,
When we know to be "contrary"
    Is a failing of the fair?

So just why it should be " Mary "
    Will my senses still perplex,
For in calling her "contrary "
    He informed us of the sex.

TO THE GIRLS IN *LIFE*.

How perfect are the gowns you wear,
   Your figures how complete ;
How finely moulded are your arms,
   How dainty are your feet.

How clever, too, your speeches are,
   How quick your repartee ;
If only you could really talk,
   And really would, with me.

I do not like those fellows, though,
   You 've with you all the time ;
They 're dangerous rivals to the men
   Whose only gift is rhyme.

How quickly could we fall in love,
   And find a charming wife,
If only girls we really knew
   Were like the girls in *Life !*

A POET'S PREDICAMENT.

ALAS for the fancy that led my pen
  In the wandering ways of rhyme !
How little I thought, when I wrote them then,
I should hate my verses so fiercely when
  I should read them in later time.

How little I knew they would prove the wreck
  Of my hopes at a future day.
I sold the verses, and cashed the check,
And spent it (I think it was Pommery Sec),
  And went on my daily way.

To-day they are published—my name signed, too—
  Distributed all over town,—
Addressed to a maiden "fond and true,"
Whose hair is " golden " and eyes are " blue "—
  And *her* hair and eyes are brown !

THE OLD NEGRO'S PRAYER.

Oh, Massa, I 'se weary an' cripple' an' ole,
But I 'se journeyin' on ter de City ob Gol';
Yo' calls li'l chillun its wonders to see,
An' sho'ly dar 's room fer ole niggers lak me.

We 's free fum de shackles we onct use ter w'ar,
But we 's nebber foun' freedom fum sorrer an' car';
De burden gits bigger de ol'er we grows,
An' mo' rougher de journey de furder we goes.

At ch'ch, ev'y Sunday, de preacher tells how
We mus' all earn our bread in de sweat ob de brow,
But we 's got roomyticks, so we kaint till de groun',
An' we ain' good fer nothin' cep' hangin' aroun'.

But, Massa, please 'member dey 's some un us blin',
An' we don't see de paf we 's a-strivin' ter fin',
And dey 's some un us deef, so we kaint hear Yo' voice,
An' we 's bent an' we 's feeble, but yit we 'll rejoice—

Fer de light 'll come back wid de Jubilee Mo'n,
An' de yeahs hear agin wid de soun' ob de ho'n,
An' de back it 'll straighten, de face 'll grow young,
An' de Heabens 'll ring wid de songs dat are sung.

An' de Lord th'u' de fiah 'll ride in His might,
Lak de sun in his glory ; an' dark 'll be light.—
Oh, Massa, we 's libin' so dat, widout feah,
When Yo' calls us by name we kin all answer "Heah ! "

WITH THE ROSES.

"Sweets to the sweet " the proverb runs.
　　If so, these are your due,—
Although they 're neither half so sweet,
　　Nor half so dear, as you !

THE VICTOR.

Whene'er the King doth hold his Court
　　The Princess is his joy and pride,
And to himself he smiles to see
　　The foreign Princes at her side.
Through all the Court a Jester moves,
　　With merry laugh and song, the while,
A thousand times repaid for all
　　If he but see the Princess smile.

And strange it is, although in state
　　Around her royal suitors throng,
With dainty words, she listens most
　　Unto the Jester's simple song.
And if a courtier catch her smile,
　　If he would turn his powdered head
He 'd see it was not meant for him,
　　But what the smiling Jester said.

Ah, Princess, it should not be hard
　　Your treasured secret to surprise,
For where the Jester moves about
　　There follow fast your watchful eyes.

Oh, foolish Princess ! Why should you,
    Entranced by all his jingling chimes,
Refuse a royal love, for one
    Whose only art is making rhymes?

Tis true his songs are all for you,
    As all his heart is yours alone,
But could you not by love have placed
    Some nobler suitor on your throne ?
Ah, dainty fops that court her smile,
    If you but knew her Fool caressed her,
How gladly would the proudest change
    His rank and wealth to be her Jester !

WITH A LACE HANDKERCHIEF.

I SEND this little bit of lace,
As emblematic of the grace
Which makes your heart its resting place,
    My gentle Mary.
You know that it has oft been told
In rhymes and tales in days of old,
There lives in every snowy fold
    A little fairy.

If this be true, I have no fears
That ever in the coming years
This lace will wipe away your tears,
    For all will love you ;
And I have charged each elfish sprite
To tell you all I wish to-night,
. And make forever fair and bright
    The sky above you.
    7

A FRIEND

DEATH is a healer whose
Visits we may not choose,
  Nor stay his call ;
Equal to rich and poor,
His is a certain cure,
  That comes to all.

He, with a gentle touch,
Soothes those who suffer much,
  Stills those who laugh—
Those who may pass the cup
Lightly that Life holds up,
  And those who quaff.

All earthly storm and strife,
Though they have wrecked a life,
  His voice can still.
Pain's heavy iron bands
Loose where he lays his hands—
  Break at his will.

Love is for life alone ;
Sorrow and sigh and moan
    Each with it blends.
Laughter and song must cease ;
Death only bringeth peace
    That never ends.

REMEMBRANCE.

No words will ever be as sweet
  As were the words she used to say.
No day will ever be as sad
  As was the one she went away.

Some other hand may rest in mine
  As through the world I slowly go,
But none will ever be as dear
  As that soft touch I used to know.

CHRISTMAS.

Oh, the glorious Christmas weather !
When all hearts keep time together,
   And we never have a feeling
      That is not serene and bright ;
When the snow is falling, falling,
And the sound of coasters calling
   To their fellows on the hillside,
      Echoes clearly through the night.

How the sleigh bells tinkle, tinkle,
While the snow goes crinkle, crinkle,
   And the furs and robes about us
      Hardly serve to keep us warm ;
And our feet and fingers tingle
To the music and the jingle,
   As we drive on swiftly homeward
      Through the thickly flying storm.

How the lights shine out to meet us !
How the dogs rush out to greet us,
   As we draw up at the gateway ;
      And the horses, in a steam,

Stand there restless, stamping, stamping
In the drifting snow, and champing
   At their bits, with white manes tossing—
      Like the shadows in a dream.

How the blazing hickory fire
Flashes higher, higher, higher,
   As we pile the wood upon it
      And draw closer all around ;
While the cracking and the snapping
Of the logs, like wood-gnomes rapping
   For release from out their prisons,
      Has a weird and wintry sound.

Oh, the warmth and love within there !
Oh, the stories that we spin there,
   To the children, of the Ice King
      Who lives out in all the snow :
But at length we leave the fable,
And recall the lowly stable
   Where the King of Love was lying,
      Many centuries ago.

Till, as we all sit there thinking,
Little eyes with sleep are blinking,
   And the old clock in the hallway
      Tells of Christmas come again ;

And the whole white earth rejoices,
As though sweet, angelic voices
  Sang again the old, old story,
    " Peace on earth, good will to men."

Then the merry early waking,
As the Christmas morn is breaking,
  Finding everybody happy
    With the warmth of Christmas cheer.
Ah, when love is such a feeling,
All our better selves revealing,
  Let us dwell in love forever,
    And have Christmas all the year !

A WISH.

IF " evil that men do lives after them,"
  I hope, sometimes,
The evil that lives after me
  May be my rhymes.

SMOKE.

As I watch the pale blue spirals
　From my brown Havana curl,
Every whiff is soft and fragrant
　As the sweet breath of a girl.

And the blue clouds, softly rising,
　In a moment turn to white,
As the light wind breaks their beauty
　And they float into the night.

And my fancies all are brighter,
　And my thoughts are sweeter far,
As though both had caught the sparkle
　And the scent of my cigar.

POLLY.

POLLY is pretty, and Polly is bright ;
Polly is witty ; her laughter is light.

Polly is winning, and Polly is fair ;
Like the beginning of morn is her hair,

Ere the sun o'er the mists mounts to the skies—
Like to their glory the blue of her eyes.

Charms that are mental as well do I find ;
Polly is gentle, but Polly 's not kind.

Polly plays lightly when love is the stake,
Caring but slightly whose heart she may break.

Mine is not lonely—she holds many hearts,
Though she laughs only at Love and his arts.

Polly, I pray you, since mine you have won,
Keep it ! Thus may you repair what you 've done.

MODERN MOTHER GOOSE.

IF the noted "Old Woman Who Lived in a Shoe"
  Should ever come back to this earth,
Commodious quarters she quickly would find
  Were Chicago the place of her birth.

While "Little Jack Horner Who sat in a Corner"
  Would feel quite at home in a seat
On the Produce Exchange, if the market were brisk,
  And he ever got "cornered" in wheat.

And "Little Boy Blue," with his fondness for sleep,
  Would be blue as the bluest Blue Ridge
If he lived in New York, but could sleep as he pleased
  If he only moved over the Bridge.

A VALENTINE.

THOUGH Cupid is a merry, careless wight,
And will not always at my bidding write
  The things that I would like to have him say,
Yet to the rogue I gave a pen and ink,
And bade him set down all that I might think,
  Or he could see within my heart to-day.

So time passed on, with many thoughts beguiled,
Till, looking up, I saw that Cupid smiled,
  And to my tongue came quickly words of blame :
But well I knew for these he would not care,
So stooped to see what he had written there.—
  On all the page I only found your name.

My first surprise I very quickly masked,
But still he smiled, and I impatient asked,
  "Why did you trifle this way ?   Tell me, sir ! "
He turned to answer me, and, open-eyed,
Looked up into my face as he replied,
  " The only thoughts you had were thoughts of her."

LOVE LETTERS.

Tom (*entering*)—Ah, burning letters?
  I 'll bet, in the flame and the smoke
There's a story, eh?

      Dick—That 's no reason
For laughing.   I don't see the joke.

Tom—Well, the first time it 's not funny.
  You 'll get used to it, though, by and by,
As I have, and—

      Dick (*very stiffly*)—
I don't think I shall, though.

         Tom—Why?

Dick—My story ends with these letters.

 Tom—Nonsense!

    Dick—Well, it is true.

Tom—Maybe, but tell me the story.

DICK—It would n't much interest you,
But nevertheless I will tell it.
  This first letter, then, is the one
That she wrote from the mountains last Summer.

  TOM (*reading*)—" I wish you could run
Up in time for the Thursday cotillion.
  Brother Jack will come too, over night.
Mamma will be happy to see you,
  And, really, I think that you might."—
Did you go ?

  DICK—Do Turks go to Mecca ?
Does a saint go to kneel at a shrine ?
Does a Christian forsake his religion ?
  Well, that girl in the mountains was mine.

TOM—You answered the letter in person ?

  DICK—I went just to stay to the ball,
But—

  TOM—With a trip to the city
Now and then, you stayed through to the Fall.

DICK—Yes, that is so.

Tom—The ending
I can guess.   She is married.

Dick—No.

Tom—Well, if she is n't, what ails you ?

Dick (*softly*)—She 's going to be, though.

Tom—Where is she now ?

Dick—In London.
She's had all the place could afford,
And is coming home now, to be married.

Tom—Of course tis no less than a lord.
I suppose he sails with them from England ?

Dick—No, for her heart was " still true
To New York," so she wrote.

Tom—She has n't
Forgotten last Summer and you ?
You tell me you hear from her ?   Come, now——

Dick (*proudly*)—Those letters were mailed
From about every city in Europe,
And to catch every steamer that sailed.

Tom—Why are you burning them all, then ?
Oh, perhaps she 's refused you ?

Dick—No ;
The last was signed " Ever yours only."

Tom—But you were burning them, though.

Dick—Yes, for their writer is coming,
Herself, and this cable—the last—
See ! (*reading it*) " Sailing, Majestic."
God grant that the passage be fast !

Tom—That is the end of the story ?

Dick (*smiling*)—Well, yes, or will be
When the steamer arrives, for you see, Tom,
She is going to be married to me.

WARNING.

Music is her laughter sweet,

And like fairy's are her feet ;

Roses find their richest hue

In her cheeks, but ye who woo,

Even though she smile on you,

Be ye ever fearful ;

Even though she doth beguile,

Linger but a little while,

Love will leave you tearful.

MAKING RHYMES.

Tis such a very pleasant thing
To hear another poet sing,
To see how easy he can fling
    The rhymes in songs and sonnets ;
But tis so hard to do, yourself,
When you, mayhap—unlucky elf—
Must ring those rhymes for sordid pelf,
    And coats and shoes and bonnets.

Somehow his verse so easy flows,
His Pegasus as freely goes
As though the minstrel really knows
    Just what is coming after ;
While mine is crippled, halts and breaks,
As though he had a thousand aches
In every joint, until he makes
    Himself a thing for laughter.

Sometimes tis hard to find a rhyme,
When you have started out to climb—

Here 's an example, just in time—
      The heights of grim Parnassus ;
For, to " Parnassus," now, you know
I need a rhyme, and searching go
Among my thoughts, which run as slow
      As—well, as cold molasses.

But that 's enough to show how hard
Must work the patient, laboring bard
To have his verse escape the card
      That tells him tis rejected—
" With thanks " of course.   Polite, you see,
But little comfort, if, like me,
Instead of thanks, an " X " or " V "
      Was what he had expected.

GRATITUDE.

IT happened that a King who lived
   When all the Kings were good,
In riding, one day, came upon
   Two beggars, in his wood.

And to the beggars straight he cried,
   " Tis well that we should meet,
For full I see your need of clothes,
   And things to drink and eat.

" Go up unto my castle, now,
   And tell him at the gate
To give each one a suit of clothes,
   Likewise a well-filled plate.

" And let him surely not forget
   To give unto each man,
In which to drink his Sovereign's health,
   A deep and foaming can."

The beggars went and quick were clothed,
  And had their drink and meat,
And then upon their way they went,
  With quite uncertain feet.

Now, mark you—beggars' natures then
  And now are quite the same—
" That chap has got no sense," laughed they ;
  " Zounds, he was easy game ! "

CUPID.

Whom Cupid hits with feathered dart
  He quick repays with kisses,
And, clever marksman though he is,
  One-half his shots are Misses.

A QUANDARY.

I KNOW two girls, both winning, sweet, and fair—
As bright as morning, but with eyes and hair
   As dark as night :
One, tall and graceful, beautiful and slender ;
The other, gentle, loving, true and tender,
   And fairy light.

'Twould puzzle any one who knew the two
To name that one to whom his fancy flew,
   And truly say
(Could he but calmly think of them apart)
If pretty little Maud had won his heart,
   Or lovely May.

AFTERNOON TEA.

THAT " There 's many a slip
'Twixt the cup and the lip,"
Is a saying that 's old, I 'll allow ;
　But in watching May tip
　Her light tea-cup and sip
From its edge, it occurred to me now,

　That if I were that cup
　She was just lifting up
To her lip—By the spirit of Puck !—
　If a slip, I declare,
　Were to happen just there,
I should think it was very hard luck !

LOTTIE.

" Oh, Lottie is fair as the morning,
  And Lottie is bright as the sun ;
Her cheeks all the roses are scorning,
  Her eyes dance with frolic and fun.

" She fills all the day with her chatter,
  With laughter the pauses between,
And care to the four winds doth scatter—
  For Lottie is merry sixteen."

But what though Miss Lottie is pretty ?
  And what though Miss Lottie is bright ?
And what though she really be witty,
  Or merry from morning till night ?

What good does it do me to know it,
  Though her presence makes Summer of Fall ?
For my brother, alas, is her poet,
  And I 've never seen her at all !

A FISH STORY.

THERE was a fisherman—But stay,
   You 'll not believe the tale I tell.
It does n't end the usual way
   That fishing stories do, but—well,
I 'll let it go for what tis worth—
   That it *were* true you all will wish—
A fisherman once walked the earth
   Who never lost the biggest fish.

IDENTIFIED.

WHO is that little man who sighs,
   And seems afraid to claim his life ?
Why, that 's the man who won the prize
   For " Hints on Managing a Wife."

HER LETTER.

AH ! here 's the answer to my note
  In which I asked her to be mine.
If she but favor what I wrote
  I 'll kneel forever at her shrine.

I wish she wrote more plainly. What ?
  Oh, yes !—" I got your note to-day,
And hasten to—to—say— " Great Scott !
  What *is* it that she hastes to say ?

" That though we were dear friends "—Of course
  I might have known 'twould end like this—
" I never thought of love."—I 'll force
  Behind me this short dream of bliss.

" So that your declaration quite
  Surprises me, I must confess.
I 'll think about it over night."—
  Well, that means " No," then.--" P. S.—Yes."

THE SOUTHLAND.

THERE the slow rivers glide down to the sea ;
There the wind quivers the vine and the tree.

There the bird voices give life to the air,
All earth rejoices, and Nature is fair.

There the shy Springtime first stops on her way,
Careless what King Time or Winter may say.

There every flower gives home to a bee ;
There every hour is happy and free.

Hearts there are truthful and friendship is dear,
Growing more youthful with love every year.

Honor a boast is, o'er all and before ;
Kindness stands hostess at each Southern door.

Breezes are blowing o'er valley and hill ;
Blossoms are snowing in memory still.

Northland is home, though, and there must I be :
Whene'er I roam, though, the Southland for me !

A MAIDEN'S "NO."

Long in secret had I worshipped
  All the beauty of her face ;
Tenderly my heart had cherished
  Every winning, girlish grace.

Till I asked, one evening, chatting
  In the fire's dancing light,
Would it very much offend her
  If I stole a kiss to-night ?

" Yes, of course," she quickly answered ;
  Adding sharply, " Don't you dare !
The impertinence to ask me !
  Why, you knew that I should care."

And she seemed so much in earnest
  That I dropped the subject quite,
And we talked of other matters
  Till the time to say good-night.

When she stood a moment, smiling,
   And she tossed her pretty head
As she looked at me, and, laughing,
   Then this little maiden said :

" That 's the way with all you fellows
   Who write silly little rhymes.
In the time you spent in asking
   You could kiss me fifty times ! "

ODE TO A DOCTOR.

THE Doctor comes, and quick prescribes ;
   And then, when we are better,
He sends a bill that reads like this :
   " To Dr. Cureall, Dr."

For when we 're in the grasp of Pain,
   And he has come and knocked her,
We surely must admit that we
   Are Dr. to our Dr.

THE GOLDEN GATE.

WHERE the waves of the Western ocean
　　Lap the shores of a golden State,
And the door to the New World's treasures
　　Is known as the Golden Gate,
I stood in the light of the sunset,
　　And afar in the Western skies
A strange and a shadowy vision
　　Passed slowly before my eyes.

There were thousands of hurrying figures,
　　As they came in the days of old,
Like the hosts of the brave Crusaders,
　　At the rallying cry of "Gold!"
How high were the hopes they cherished,
　　Of the ease of a future life;
How many the dreams that perished
　　In the tumult of toil and strife.

How many a weary pilgrim
　　Died, cursing the mocking Fate
That had led his feet from the hearthstone
　　Through the arch of the Golden Gate!

And the sea, as it sighed around me,
   Told tales of the long ago,—
Of the ships with their souls and treasure,
   That came with its ebb and flow ;

Of the last sad, lingering partings
   Whenever a vessel sailed ;
How many a heart had broken,
   How many a spirit quailed ;
How bitter the hopeless anguish
   Since some remembered date,
When the hopes and the lives of thousands
   Sailed out through the Golden Gate ;

Of the patient and weary watchers
   That stood on the Western shore
And waited a missing vessel,
   And prayed for the souls it bore ;
Of the thankful and glad rejoicing
   When, with all of its priceless freight,
The barque that they thought had foundered
   Came in through the Golden Gate.

But the vision was slowly changing,—
   And there, where the red sun dips,
Stood a city in whose proud harbor
   Was anchored a world of ships :

And I turned in the gathering darkness
From my vision of Time and Fate,
As the rays of the fading sunlight
Shone faint through the Golden Gate.

TO LOVE.

Oh, Love, thy changing will breaks many a heart ;
Thy tyrant spell all souls must own, and yet
One will have long forgotten ere they part,
And one will love and never can forget.

One's gentle trust and perfect faith are hurled
From Heaven's heights to depths as deep as Hell ;
While one goes lightly smiling through the world,
Again to weave, again to break the spell.

AN IDEA.

IF I could only write a rhyme
    With some new joke hid in it,
To catch the editorial eye
    As soon as he 'd begin it,

I 'd send it out with gleeful heart,
    My full name to it signing,
Well knowing it was different from
    The ones he 'd been declining.

Of course he might not read the rhyme—
    They sometimes don't—but should one,
I 'd like to have him laugh and say,
    " By George, but that 's a good one ! "

And when his mirth had died away,
    , And he was more collected,
I 'd like to have him send a card
    That would not read—" Rejected."

But editors are hard to please.
    They never laugh—I know 'em—
Unless they laugh that I should think
    This one that kind of poem.

"EVER YOURS."

It lies before me as I write,
And though I turn, my wandering sight
    Again it quick allures—
A plain and modest little note,
From which in fancy oft I quote
     The ending—"Ever yours."

And as I watch it where it lies,
Her waving hair and soft blue eyes
    My memory quickly brings ;
And, like a picture, to my mind
Come blushing cheeks and glances kind,
    And other pleasant things :

While to myself I frankly own
My heart is hers, and hers alone—
    I worship at her shrine,
And think how different life would seem
If she of whom I fondly dream
    Were really—ever mine !

But she, alas, ne'er wrote it there
With half a thought that I would care.
    She 's a stenographer—
My brother's—thus it was, you see,
That she wrote " Ever yours," for he
    Dictated it to her.

REVISED.

" TIS money makes the mare go "—
    A proverb oft you 've heard ;
But that was in the olden time,
    And now it seems absurd.

For if you go and put a bet
    On any mare you know,
'Instead of money making her,
    She 'll make the money go !

MY LADY.

My Lady has no ancestral hall,
With its oaken floor and its gilded wall ;
No pages start at her beck and call,
　　To quickly serve My Lady.

No maids of honor around her stand,
No knights and vassals wait her command,
No signet graces the slender hand
　　Of her I call My Lady.

She owns no acres, nor jewels rare,
For her only wealth is her golden hair,
And who wins her hand holds her fortune there—
　　Would it were I, My Lady !

No title descends in her family line,
But peace and truth in her clear eyes shine,
And she lives a queen by a right divine,
　　And reigns by love, My Lady !

LYRA.

OH, yes, Lyra, you are fair—
From the shining golden hair
That has crowned you, down to where
    Dainty feet are peeping.
Yes, your eyes are soft and bright—
Stars in many a lover's night—
May their tender, liquid light
    Ne'er be dimmed by weeping.

Oh, your mirror tells you true.
Trust it, Lyra.   Why need you,
As you often love to do,
    Stand so long before it?
Think you it withholds a part,
Does not truly use its art?—
Could it show your inmost heart
    How I would adore it!

Have not lovers cried your praise,
Poets sung you in their lays,
Are not all your pretty ways
    Known and loved and noted?

Are not all your speeches caught
By quick ears, and every thought,
Though it may amount to naught,
     If you say it, quoted?

By the fame of Venus' dove,
Little wonder that you love,
In your dainty bower above,
     To stand before your mirror.
See you there, as others do,
All that 's sweet and pure and true,
All the soul that 's shining through
     Your fair beauty, Lyra?

A FANCY.

IF by some magic spell or trick,
     We all could be the ones
We most admire, think how thick
     Would be Joe Jeffersons!

CHRISTMAS EVE.

THE self-same stars shine clear to-night,
   Across the glistening snow,
That smiled on peaceful Bethlehem
   Two thousand years ago.

Oh, Prince of Peace, though we may stray
   Far from Thy gracious ways,
At Christmas time we all come back,
   As in the younger days ;

And 'round the open fireplace
   Are children once again,
And sing the song of Peace on earth
   And good will unto men.

And though it passes with the night,
   We 're better all the year,
That for one day our hearts were filled
   With love and Christmas cheer.

AN UNPOPULAR MAN.

"But why, my dear," her mother said,
    "Do you refuse his offers?
There 's many a girl would give her head
    To own one-half his coffers."

"I do not like him," she replied.
    "But why?" The maid explains,
"No girl would like him—I have tried.
    Why, Mother, he has brains!"

IF SHE WISHES TO.

"If woman can make
    The worst wilderness dear,"
She can even make life
    Worth the living, just here.

THE EIGHTEENTH BIRTHDAY.

My little friend, pray pardon me
    A few familiar lines,
And if I seem presumptuous, think
    That friendship, like new wines,.

May much improve with age, tis said,
    And grow in strength with time —
For on that plea I venture now
    To write you this poor rhyme.

May you have every joy you wish
    That youth and love can give ;
And may you, living out your life,
    Teach others how to live.

May all your future days be full
    Of happiness and light,
And may a guiding star of hope
    Shine clear in every night.

May all your life, both night and day,
    Be free from grief or tears,
And may you count me still your friend,
    At *double* eighteen years.

BEYOND.

To sleep, but never more to wake
 To this sad life, and know
Its love or longing, joy or grief,
 Its struggle and its woe ;
To pass to brighter, fairer scenes,
 From calm and peaceful sleep,
And never more know throb of pain,
 Nor find a cause to weep :
If dying be to gain all this,
 To lose naught but the breath
That binds to mortal life,—oh, what
 Has man to fear from Death ?

GHOSTS OF THE HEART.

In each man's heart a phantom dwells,
  There darkly comes and goes,
Of her who should have blessed his life,
  But brought him only woes.

Sometimes he seems to feel the clasp
  Of shadowy jewelled fingers ;
Sometimes a sweet, angelic face
  Within his memory lingers.

Dark thoughts may shroud the ghostly form
  And hide her like a pall,
But once he thought her smiling face
  The fairest face of all.

No matter when their pathways crossed,
  Fair May or bleak December,
That woman rules his life the most
  Whom he must thus remember.

HEARTS.

THEY played a game the other night,
   In which I had a part ;
A game in which that person wins
   Who does not take a heart.

I nearly took them all, and lost
   The game, of course, but—well,
Now, who could win a game of Hearts
   Against a girl like Belle ?

And though she plays as good a game
   Of Hearts as well could be,
She also lost, that night, because
   She won my heart from me.

RHYME AND REASON.

I 'LL ne'er be slave to any,
　　I 'll bow the knee to none ;
In faith, I love too many,
　　To bind myself to one.

For faces made for smiling,
　　Will often wear a frown ;
And blue eyes, though beguiling,
　　Are not more so than brown.

So when one maiden chances
　　To frown, I 'll seek the while
Some other maiden's glances,
　　Until she choose to smile.

But if mayhap I marry,
　　And she be frowning then,
With her I have to tarry
　　Until she smiles again.

A THANKSGIVING RHYME.

Oh, Thanksgiving Day is coming,
  But unthankful is the writer
Who is penning stories on it,
  Or is forced to be inditer
Of a gobble-gobble sonnet
  To the turkey, and to greet him
With a seasonable epic
  Ere we season him and eat him.

For it 's not an easy matter
  Writing rhythmic rhymes to order,
But the poet never quibbles,
  For a poet can't afford a
Life in which he only scribbles.
  Has he turkey, work must bring him ;
But I 'd rather be the turkey
  Than the poet who must sing him.

AN IDYL OF SUMMER.

ALL Summer she threw her
 Own charm on the shore,
But the ocean that knew her
 Now knows her no more.

As the belle of the ball, now,
 She whirls in the waltz ;
Who would not risk all now ?
 She ne'er can be false.

For the love of the Summer
 Burns true in her heart,
And I ne'er shall part from her
 Till death do us part.

A TYPE.

He was faultless in dress, and was dapper and small ;
  With his manners the girls were quite struck ;
He was friendly on very short notice, with all,
  And he had the most wonderful luck.

On the races it never had failed him, he said.
  He won seven hundred, or eight,
On a horse that the rest of the people thought " dead,"
  But he backed him at 10 to 1 straight.

With winnings at poker his pockets were stored—
  His luck made him certain to win,
And he always had all of the chips on the board
  When the time came at last to cash in.

Or he just took a flyer in C. B. & Q.—
  He often made turns on the Street,
And was more than successful, or so he told you,
  On Chicago's last corner in wheat.

He may have been truthful—be that as it might,
  He was most unaccountably floored
When his landlady asked him, on Saturday night,
  For a ten-dollar bill for his board.

CINDERELLA.

She claims the sweetest songs I sing,
　In every kind of metre :
They flow like music from my heart,
　That trembles when I greet her.

One charm she has, too slight to catch
　In rhymes however airy,
And much I fear 't was rifled from
　Some poor unlucky fairy.

And so I proudly sing the praise
　Of all her other graces,
But leave unsung the little feet
　That hide beneath her laces.

. For though of nothing could I write
　That 's daintier or sweeter,
They never could fill any verse,
　However short its metre.
　　　10

A SPRING BLOSSOM.

THOUGH Southern suns are kind,'I know,
   I never should suppose
So early in the Spring could blow
   So sweet a Texas rose.

May you find this new world a place
   Of beauty everywhere,
And may you grow to every grace—
   Be gentle, good, and fair.

Gallant is every Southern son ;
   But though they 're brave and true,
I hope that I, a Northern one,
   May favor find with you.

METEMPSYCHOSIS.

I KNOW I 've lived before : at times
   Come gleams of that existence,
Like distant bells, in broken chimes,
   With sweet and strange persistence.

Half-glimpses of a girl I knew
   Are visions that are strongest,
And waken memories fond and true,
   That stay with me the longest.

I cannot tell how long ago
   It is since first I met her
In stately minuet and slow—
   But I can ne'er forget her.

And though these nineteenth-century days
   Bring happy scenes before me,
At times I walk in other ways,
   And their old spell comes o'er me.

I seem to wrap her in her cloak,
  With its pure swan's-down lining ,
I know that when of love I spoke
  She laughed at all my pining.

I wrote her sonnets by the yard,
  With Cupid as my tutor ;
Alas, she scorned the humble bard,
  To wed a princely suitor.

To-night I 've met her here, the same
  As then, in that cotillion !
And though she bears a different name,
  I 'd know her in a million.

Again the love that claimed my rhymes,
  Through all my soul is stealing ;
Again, as in long vanished times,
  At her dear feet I 'm kneeling.

I love her as I loved her then—
  And, by the great Lord Harry !
No princes need apply again :
  For that 's the girl I 'll marry !

A LAWYER'S BRIEF.

WHEN dying men, in drawing wills,
  Their chattels to convey,
Omit some words, the law ofttimes
  Implies what they would say.

If, then, in giving you my love,
  Some words are lacking, still
It should be given due effect,
  According to the will.

When in the law some solemn act
  A man intends to do,
He stamps the paper with his seal ;
  And so, when I to you

Words cannot write, you still may know
  All that I really feel,
By thinking of that point of law,
  And looking at this seal.

A LITERARY HISTORY.

ONE day I wrote a little skit,
    In rather clever verse,
In hopes a *Life* of rhyme and wit
    Would help to fill my purse.

I prospered, but not growing rash
    Like many another youth,
Who only writes for sordid cash,
    I also wrote for *Truth*.

And then, much like some other men
    Who find themselves in luck,
Love in light verse ran from my pen,
    Inspired, of course, by *Puck*.

For him I wrote both night and day—
    The laughing, happy rogue—
Love songs and sonnets light and gay,
    That soon were much in *Vogue*.

Flushed with success, I looked on wine.
   When brought to justice, " Fudge ! "
I only cried, and paid my fine
   With jokes that caught the *Fudge*.

Then *Harpers* sung my songs, and now
   It is my fate to be
A poet, critics must allow,
   Of this last *Century*.

A CATASTROPHE.

CONFOUND that girl !   All my cigars
   She 's spilled upon the shelf,
And mixed up those I give my friends
   With those I smoke myself.

A SEPTEMBER GREETING.

A HEARTY welcome home again,
　　Old friend from Morris Cove ;
You don't know how we 've missed you here—
　　We really have, by Jove !

I 've heard your name at all the clubs
　　A dozen times a day ;
Our suppers have n't seemed the same—
　　At least to me—since May.

But now you 're with us once again
　　Our pleasures are complete.
And so plump, too !　Why, I declare,
　　You 're good enough to eat !

MEMORIES.

Though I have lived since last we met
   'Mid many climes and men,
Set in a hazy frame of years
   I see your face again.

When last we parted—how, you know,
   As I do far too well—
I found in Europe what you made
   My life to me—a hell!—

Monaco, where they soon complete
   What girls like you 've begun,
And where on single turns of cards
   A fortune 's lost or won.

And as I there watched wretched men
   Stake all on one last throw,
Came back to me that other game
   We played so long ago ;

How in that game of love, where I
    Risked all for your dear sake,
You played as carelessly as though
    My life were not the stake.

And how with all your winning smiles—
    God ! what each one had cost !—
You calmly told me at the last
    The life I staked—was lost.

I wonder if there never comes
    Across your careless life
One thought of him who lost his all
    In that unequal strife ;

If even you, so falsely cold,
    Can ever quite forget ;
If you have never walked within
    The shadow of regret.

But vain these mem'ries. Those who sleep
    Beneath the deepest sea
Are not more dead to friends they loved
    Than you are dead to me.

BETWEEN THE LINES.

Her little note is folded neat,
And dainty is the written sheet,
With just before her name so sweet—
    " Sincerely yours."

I know that you will coolly say
She signs her letters in that way
To friends (my rivals too) each day—
    " Sincerely yours."

I know quite well the phrase is old,
And rather formal, too, and cold,
And yet I think the truth it told—
    " Sincerely yours."

And it has given grace to me
To ask my darling to agree
Through all her life to really be
    Sincerely mine !

WHEN LOVE IS OLD.

THE World seems old and cold to Love,
   When Love is blithe and young ;
It cannot share his careless mirth,
   And does not speak his tongue.

But with the growth of added years
   Love gains in wisdom too,
And takes no pleasure in his tricks,
   As once he used to do.

He 's then content with simpler joys
   Than those his youth would find
In making lovers seem untrue
   And maidens prove unkind.

And in the calm, serene delights
   That happy years unfold,
The World seems young and bright to Love,
   When Love himself is old.

ABSENT AND PRESENT.

WHEN I am absent from her side
  My thoughts are most unkind,
And jealousies, a cruel tide,
  Sweep in upon my mind.

I envy every sunbeam then
  That dares to kiss her cheeks,
The smile she gives it back again,
  And every word she speaks ;

The lightest breath of summer winds
  That plays about her hair,
And every passing joy she finds
  Or knows when I 'm not there.

But she has grace such thoughts to heal,
  For when my brow and hair
The magic of her fingers feel,
  I bid farewell to care.

Her smile is sunshine, and her voice
   Like music to my ear ;
My heart doth quicken and rejoice,
   To know that she is near.

No mighty monarch on his throne
   Could find such joy and pride,
As I, when she, my Queen, my own,
   Once more is by my side.

AN UNWILLING SCHOLAR.

O'ER all her sisters fond and fair,
   That one I place above,
And seek to find her everywhere,
   Who ne'er has learned to love.

Though I am very much afraid,
   If such a girl there be,
That when I chance to find the maid,
   She will not learn from me.

FAREWELL TO YOUTH.

Well, good-bye !   Farewell, my Youth !
We were happy friends, forsooth.
Merry days we 've spent together,
In the springtime's sunny weather ;
Laughed more often than we cried,
Sang more often than we sighed ;
Had our share of love and pleasure,
Quaffed them from a brimming measure ;
Shared them always, you and I.—
Now you leave me.   Well, good-bye !

I shall not forget you, Youth.
Though your faith and hope and truth
From my life you lightly sever,
I shall mourn and miss you ever ;
Still shall hold your memory dear
Many a long and weary year.
Parting words are quickly spoken ;
Ties of years are slowly broken.
Well we wove them, you and I.
Once again, my Youth, good-bye !

A BIRTHDAY.

DEAR Mother, let us pause to-day,
   While time is flying fast,
To drink a health to coming years,
   Remembrance to the past.

Remembrance, though, to those alone
   That brought you happy days ;
Forgetfulness to those of grief,
   In memory's tender haze—

That half-forgetfulness that time
   ·Throws 'round life's sadder parts,—
So that, although remembered, yet
   They do not break our hearts.

And though the sands of life each year
   Run faster, may you find
A thousand pleasures yet to come,
   And all your griefs behind :

Like to a traveller on a hill,
   The blue sky bending o'er him,
With only half his journey done,
   The fairest stretched before him.

And since we do not wish to think
   That each succeeding one
Will steal away a happy year
   From those we 've yet to run,

We 'll not keep time as others do,
   But try a better way :
In each bright day we 'll live a year,
   Count every year a day.

THE LESSON OF THE YEARS.

In youth we long for Time to run
  With flying feet life's pleasant ways ;
No sooner does one day of bliss
Pass into night's long loneliness,
Than Youth, with his impatient sight,
Is watching for the coming light
        Of other happy days.

But when the years are slowly gone,
  And all the hopes they brought are dead,
Ah, then it is we learn, at last,
That all too soon the years have past,
With all their thoughts and mem'ries sweet,—
That all too quickly ran Time's feet,
        With softly falling tread.

AT THE PORTAL.

DEATH has no terrors, fears, nor pains,
  From Life to bar my way :
I go as from Siberian plains
  To gardens of Cathay.

www.ingramcontent.com/pod-product-compliance
Lightning Source LLC
Chambersburg PA
CBHW031114020726
47495CB00007B/2191